Washington, D.C.
1864

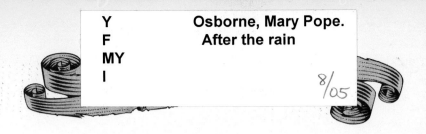

After the Rain

Virginia's Civil War Diary

· Book Two ·

by Mary Pope Osborne

Scholastic Inc. New York

November 2, 1864

In a little while, our train will arrive in Washington City — or "Mr. Lincoln's Washington," as Pa calls it.

Much of our trip has been lovely. All the leaves are changing. Bright reds and yellows flash by.

Our lives are changing, too. We are moving from Gettysburg to Washington City. Pa and Jed are finding new jobs.

Best of all, Jane Ellen is changing — she is going to have a baby in April! She says that we must call the baby "our baby," for it will belong not just to her and Jed — but to me and Pa, as well. Imagine, in a few months, I will be a ten-year-old aunt!

I must close now and comfort Jane Ellen. The movement of the train is making her feel a bit sick.

Later

It is near midnight. We are only minutes away from Washington City. I can hardly wait to see Jed.

Jane Ellen and I have been worried about him. Two weeks ago, he came here ahead of us. He was planning to start his new job and find us a home.

In that time, he has only written two letters. In neither did he mention his work or where we would live. I fear this means he is unhappy.

Pa and Jane Ellen are talking about

President Lincoln now. They desperately hope he will be reelected next week. Jane Ellen thinks President Lincoln is the only man in the world who can put an end to slavery forever.

November 3, 1864

When Jed met us at the station, all three of us hugged him at the same time. Then we rode a buggy through the dark rain to our new home.

Jed has found a house that has three small rooms and a small kitchen. We get our water outside.

Jed and Jane Ellen have a bedroom that is hardly bigger than a horse stall. Pa has a small room, too, and I sleep on the sofa in the parlor.

Jed said he feared we would be disappointed. But we quickly assured him we were not.

I fear Jed is the one who has been sorely

disappointed. When he arrived here two weeks ago, he discovered his friend, Mr. Hoke, was away gathering war news about General Sherman. Mr. Hoke was not here to help Jed get a job as a reporter. Since the paper was in great need of someone to set type, Jed was given that job.

Jane Ellen urged Jed to telegraph Mr. Hoke about his complaints. But Jed won't. He says Mr. Hoke has far more important concerns at the moment.

I am shivering with cold now. I had better close so I can cover my head with my blanket.

November 4, 1864

Again this morning, Jed said he was sorry about our shabby rooms. He hopes he will be given a reporter's job within the month. Then we can all move to a nicer house.

Pa said he was not unhappy in the least, for he will get a job very soon. Pa wants to play his violin at one of Washington City's theaters.

I told Jed and Pa that no matter what happens, I will not be disappointed. This is a great adventure, I told them. Jane Ellen put on her most cheerful face, too.

Later

A cold rain falls outside.

Jed has gone to the newspaper. Pa has set out to look for work.

After they left, Jane Ellen and I stared out the parlor window without speaking. All we could see were shabby wooden buildings and a muddy street.

We saw many Negro people walk by. They have come to Washington in search of freedom from slavery.

Confederate deserters and bandaged Union soldiers also straggled by. They fought for different armies, but they all looked much the same — sad and weary. Both sides are desperate for the war's end.

Jane Ellen finally broke our gloomy silence. She said that she and I should be very grateful, for we are luckier than most.

Evening

I have just lit the gas lamps. Pa and Jed should be home soon.

This afternoon, Jane Ellen helped me with geography and arithmetic. She will teach me until we can afford a real school.

After our lessons, she and I scrubbed our small rooms. While we scrubbed, Jane Ellen became sick. I urged her to go back to bed.

I must confess I worry a great deal about Jane Ellen. She says her daily sickness is a natural part of carrying a baby. I know that is true. But the fact is that my mother died when I was born. And that, I think, is why I worry so.

November 5, 1864

The presidential election is only three days away. Tonight President Lincoln's supporters carried torches through the streets and cheered for him.

The race between the President and General McClellan is heating up. McClellan wants peace with the South, even if it means that slavery will not end. President Lincoln wants to end slavery *forever*.

November 6, 1864

We went to a small church on P Street. Then we bought fresh bread at the bakery. Jane Ellen and I made a good dinner of bread, potatoes, and roasted chicken.

All the gray afternoon, a fire blazed in the hearth. Pa played his violin. Jed read from *The Death of King Arthur*. We are in sore need of a new book. We have read this one so many times.

But it was wonderful for all of us to be together. We need nothing more — except our baby to be born healthy in the spring.

November 7, 1864

It was drizzly again today. Jane Ellen and I are quite nervous about the election tomorrow. After my Latin lesson, we were restless for a walk. So we carried umbrellas down Pennsylvania Avenue.

We passed boardinghouses, grocery shops, saloons, and restaurants.

We passed peddlers selling fish and newsboys selling war news.

We passed geese and hogs and cows and sheep.

We were almost to the President's mansion when it began thundering and lightning. We turned back and slogged home through a sea of mud.

Ambulance wagons plowed by us. They sloshed the mud all over our skirts. By the time we were home, our boots and clothes were nearly ruined.

I do not complain, though. The soldiers in the wagons were far more forlorn than we.

Later

Sick and wounded soldiers lie in hospitals all around the city, Jed says. He told us that President Lincoln sometimes visits them. The President goes from man to man, touching each, and saying, "God bless you."

The President has no concern for his personal safety, Jed says.

November 8, 1864
Before dawn

It pours rain outside. I am wide awake.

The election is today. I am trembling with nerves. President Lincoln is my greatest hero. Ever since I saw him speak in Gettysburg, I've felt he has been touched by the hand of God.

I worry, though, that the muddy streets

might keep his supporters away. He has many enemies, Jed says, who wish he would not be reelected.

Afternoon

Pa said crowds of men are making their way through the foggy, wet streets. Many have rolled up their trousers to wade through the mud. They all seem determined to vote.

At dinner, Jed said that Lincoln supporters are gathering outside the telegraph office to wait for the voting count.

I begged Pa to take me there. And he has said yes! He and Jed and I will leave soon, so we can hear the news with the crowd.

Evening

We have won! President Lincoln has been reelected. Hurrah!

The vote has not been completely counted. But outside the telegraph office, word came that the President has most certainly won.

The cheering crowd marched through the streets of Mr. Lincoln's Washington.

We marched straight to the President's House. Standing on his lawn, we sang "The Battle Cry of Freedom."

Soon President Lincoln and his wife appeared at a window. Through the mist, he seemed a dream figure — tall, dignified, dressed in a black suit. He made a short speech, giving thanks to the Almighty.

Pa, Jed, and I nearly danced home through the foggy, rainswept streets. Right now, as it starts to grow light, I still cannot sleep.

Isn't it amazing? We live only a short distance from the President of the United States!

This city is dirty and muddy. Our rooms are small and shabby. Pa has not found a job yet. Jed needs a raise. Jane Ellen is sick. But at this moment, there is nowhere on earth I would rather be.

November 10, 1864

Pa looked for work today at Ford's New Theatre and Grover's National Theatre. But the managers of both said that they do not need a violin player now.

November 12, 1864

Today Pa went to the Washington Theater and the Oxford Hall of Music, looking for a job. But neither of them needs a violin player, either.

Monday he will go to Seaton Hall where they have fancy balls.

I can tell Pa is beginning to get very worried. I know he fears we will not have enough money to stay here in Washington City.

November 14, 1864

Pa came home sad again. He did not get a job at Seaton Hall.

November 15, 1864

Pa has given up hope of finding work as a violin player. He read in the paper today that they need a watchman at the navy yard. He will go there tomorrow.

November 16, 1864

Jed came home with big news about the war tonight. General Sherman has led 60,000 men against Atlanta! They burned the city and left it in ruins.

November 17, 1864

Pa did not get a job at the navy yard.

Unless he gets a job, we will end up in the poorhouse, he said tonight.

Jed told Pa not to worry. He said he will quit his work at the newspaper. He said he saw an ad for a woodcutter today. And he can make more money chopping wood than setting type, he told Pa.

Pa got furious. He said Jed could not leave the newspaper — he must stay there until he uses his talents to write!

Jed said he would rather be a woodcutter.

Pa said, "Hogwash! You will not be a woodcutter, and that is final."

Pa went into his room and slammed his door.

Then Jed went into his room and slammed his door.

Jane Ellen and I just sat in the parlor and stared gloomily at the torn wallpaper.

November 18, 1864

Pa took the job as a woodcutter. He will chop firewood for the shops on Pennsylvania Avenue. Pa is not very hardy-looking. But his arms are quite strong from playing the violin.

November 21, 1864

Jed says that General Sherman's army is still in Georgia. The newspaper has sent most of its reporters to the South to cover the story.

I know Jed aches to go with them. But for once I am glad that he only sets type. I dread his ever being captured again, as he was during the Battle of Gettysburg. He still has a bad limp from his wound. And he still carries dark memories that time does not seem to erase.

This darkness causes Jed to worry a lot. Ever since the election, he has been worried about President Lincoln's safety. He has been brooding lately about the souvenir seekers who swarmed the White House after the President won. They stole tassels from window curtains. They snipped pieces from the wallpaper and chair covers.

November 23, 1864

At dinner, Jed said that President Lincoln has declared the last Thursday of every November as a national Day of Thanksgiving.

On this day, every year, we Americans will stop work and thank God for our blessings.

November 24, 1864

Today Jed and Pa stayed home to celebrate the Day of Thanksgiving.

Jed said that over 100,000 turkeys and chickens are to be served to General Grant's army today. We do not have enough money for a turkey. Lately, we are mostly eating beans for dinner, beans with a bit of bread.

While we ate our beans today, Jed talked again about President Lincoln's safety. He says the President must have more bodyguards.

While Jed worried about President Lincoln, I worried about Jane Ellen. During dinner, she became ill and had to lie down.

While I worried about Jane Ellen, Pa worried about keeping his job as a woodcutter. He fears he is not strong enough.

I hope God forgives us for not being very thankful this Thanksgiving.

November 30, 1864

Though none of us seems happy, we do have a daily routine now. Every morning Pa and Jed leave for work. Jane Ellen gives me two hours of lessons. Then she and I sew, clean, and cook. If she feels well, we shop in the market.

In the afternoon, Jane Ellen lies down, while I study my lessons.

The sky grows gray quite early, and our rooms become cold and damp. While Jane

Ellen sleeps, I sometimes feel that something awful is about to happen. I try to shake off the feeling by singing.

My spirits lift when Jane Ellen lights the lamps, and Pa and Jed come home.

December 1, 1864

Something bad has happened. It is not truly awful, though, for no one has died. Pa hurt his back chopping wood. Jed had to help him home and put him to bed.

"Now what can I do?" is all Pa can say. "Now what can I do?"

December 3, 1864

Jane Ellen and I tried to feed Pa today. But he said he could not eat. He is in despair. He fears he will not be able to do any kind of work for many days. Pa said we made a mistake in moving to Washington City. This made Jed feel bad. He left the house, even though it was raining.

Jane Ellen felt ill and went to bed.

I am sitting alone in the cold, damp parlor, shivering from worry. "Now what can I do?" I keep asking myself.

December 4, 1864

I have the answer. I will find work. Why not? Jane Ellen is too tired to give me lessons every day. We are too poor for me to go to school.

Tomorrow I will look in the *Evening Star* for a job for a ten-year-old girl. I dare not tell anyone until I find something I can do.

December 6, 1864

Each night I study the newspaper that Jed brings home.

I have only seen ads for errand boys, newspaper boys, and stable boys. Is there nothing for girls?

December 7, 1864

Today I finally saw an ad looking for a girl. It said "Girl for General Housework."

I would rather run errands, sell newspapers, or take care of horses any day than do general housework. But I have no choice.

When Pa and Jane Ellen take their afternoon naps, I will hurry to the house on Pennsylvania Avenue and apply for the job.

I will pretend to be a lady when I am interviewed. I will try to use the manners my mother would have used. Pa always says my mother was a lovely lady, a real Southern belle.

Later afternoon

I have a job!

I went to a beautiful house with stone steps. A widow named Mrs. Porter lives there. Though she has two servants already, she needs a girl to do light housekeeping. She will pay fifty cents a day!

I told her that I was the girl for the job. I said it simply, but without any doubt. I spoke in a most polite, but firm way.

Mrs. Porter laughed and said she liked my manners and my confidence.

Now I must use that confidence to tell the others about my new job. I am waiting for Pa and Jane Ellen to wake up from their naps, and for Jed to come home.

Late evening

Pa said no. Jane Ellen said no. Jed said no, too.

After they'd all said no, I gathered them together. I reminded them that I am not a child. I reminded them that I am a girl who has seen the Battle of Gettysburg. I am a girl who has ridden a horse through the torn countryside and who has visited war hospitals.

They *must* let me work for Mrs. Porter — or they will insult my courage and my dignity, I said.

Pa, Jed, and Jane Ellen all looked at one another and started to laugh.

What could they say after my speech but yes?

December 8, 1864

Today I dusted and ironed for Mrs. Porter. I sewed a torn pocket and darned a sock.

Mrs. Porter's house has a beautiful parlor and sitting room, gas and water, a large yard, an icehouse, and a carriage house. She has two funny cats named Isabel and Lydia. They scamper everywhere and like to sleep in her lap.

Mrs. Porter is very kind. She laughs a lot and moves about like a busy bee.

I am happy. I confess I prefer working in Mrs. Porter's bright, warm house to sitting alone in our cold parlor.

December 12, 1864

I love walking to Mrs. Porter's house in the early morning. The paper says it is the coldest

December for many years, but I don't mind. The city air crackles with excitement.

Through the lamplit dark, newsboys shout out, "Extra! Extra! Sherman marching through Georgia!"

Carriage horses clippity-clop over the rough cobblestones. Geese waddle. Goats and hogs wander about in the early mist.

Soon the gas lamps all go out. The bright cold sun rises over Washington City. And a fresh new day is revealed, like a new child, alive and kicking.

December 13, 1864

Jed told me that when I walk to work, I should keep an eye out for President Lincoln's carriage. He is often seen riding about the city with his son, Tad.

How will I recognize the carriage? I asked.

Jed said the President travels with about thirty soldiers on horseback. Their sabers are drawn and held over their shoulders.

Jed said that the guard was posted against President Lincoln's wishes. The President pays no mind to the fact he has many enemies.

There are even days, Jed said, when the President carelessly rides out in the open, on the back of his own gray horse. Young Tad rides by his side.

Oh, I would give anything to see President Lincoln and Tad ride down the street on horseback!

December 14, 1864

Each day my job gets better. Mrs. Porter likes me to read to her. I love to read, so this is a joy for me as well. Sometimes I read from the Bible. Or I read from William Shakespeare or Sir Walter Scott.

When I get home, I try to cheer everyone by telling them the news of my day. I even tell them about the stories I read to Mrs. Porter.

December 16, 1864

Yesterday I began reading *Swiss Family Robinson* to Mrs. Porter. I must say it is an exciting story.

At home, Pa is still unable to move about. Jane Ellen is growing bigger and still feels sick. Jed is restless about his work, aching to go to Georgia to gather news stories about General Sherman.

Tonight I tried to cheer them all by telling them about *Swiss Family Robinson*. I told them we were not unlike the Robinson family, washed up on a strange shore. We must try to make the best of everything. After all, we at least have a roof over our heads and beans every night for dinner.

December 17, 1864

Tonight I told everyone more about *Swiss Family Robinson*. That brave family has just moved into a tree house! They are planting gardens and hunting and fishing. That should give us strength, I said. If they can survive on a desert island, we can surely survive in Washington City!

Jane Ellen laughed and said I should have been a preacher. She said I am very inspiring.

December 18, 1864

Soon I will tell my family new stories — stories about Mrs. Porter's grandchildren! They are coming to visit from New York City for the Christmas holidays. I can hardly wait. I confess I have missed being with other children. These days I feel more like a grown-up than a ten-year-old girl.

December 19, 1864

Hurrah! Tomorrow Robert, Sarah, and Eliza Porter will arrive. Sarah and Eliza are eleven-year-old twins, and Robert is my age. Their father is an important lawyer in New York City.

I cannot wait to hear about their life and tell them all about mine. I can tell them about the Battle of Gettysburg and about Jed, Pa, and Jane Ellen.

I might even tell them that my mother was a Southern belle. I'll tell them she lived in Virginia, and she had two younger brothers whom I've never met. Those brothers might be fighting for the Confederacy now! My uncles could be Rebs, imagine! I'll tell them.

Maybe they'll invite me to visit them in New York City. I feel that tomorrow is the beginning of a great new adventure.

December 20, 1864

I did not actually get to visit with the Porter children today. I was dusting when they arrived. They did not speak to me. They were so excited to see their grandmother. They ran through the house shouting and laughing and chasing the cats. Their pretty mother wore a fur coat. The father and Robert wore handsome cloaks. Sarah and Eliza wore ribbons in their long, shiny hair.

Mrs. Porter introduced them to me. But they did not seem to take notice. Surely that was because they were so excited to see their grandmother.

December 21, 1864

It snowed last night.

I only briefly laid eyes on the Porter children today. They left early with their parents. They rode off in a sleigh with bells. When they returned, I heard Robert telling Mrs. Porter all about the Monticello Dining Room. They had ice cream and sugar cookies there.

The girls told her about shopping at

DeLarue's. They bought lilac ribbons for their hair and Paris kid gloves.

Again, they did not seem to take notice of me. When Robert ran down the hall, chasing the cats, I laughed. But I couldn't seem to catch his eye. When he bumped into me, he did not even say "pardon."

I felt like a girl made of air.

December 22, 1864

Today I felt again as if I were made of air. The Porter children moved about me, never catching my eye.

Is this how all servants feel? What about slaves? I cannot imagine how slaves must feel. Why, what if the Porter children "owned" me! They might even beat me, if I didn't do what they wanted!

My heart was heavy when I came home. I

did not talk to my family at all. Our rooms seem shabbier than ever.

Poison has entered my heart. I wish to be one of the Porter children and not myself.

And why not? Ice cream and sugar cookies are far better than beans. And I would love lilac ribbons for my hair.

December 23, 1864

Today the Porter children sat in the dining room while I polished the silver in the parlor. They ate preserved peaches and pears. They talked about their great adventure last night. They went to Ford's New Theatre and saw *Rip Van Winkle*. They talked about how funny and amazing it was. None of them spoke a word to me.

When I came home, I was quite cross. At dinner, I sighed and said I wish I could see a play at Ford's New Theatre someday. Pa said it cost too much to go to the theater. I blurted out that I was sick to death of being poor.

Pa looked away. He seemed hurt and surprised. Jane Ellen seemed surprised, too. I excused myself from the table, saying I was too tired to eat a plate of old beans again. "Why can't we ever have peaches or pears?" I said.

I felt ashamed lying on the sofa. I tried to talk my way out of it. I told myself I'm tired of being the cheerful one all the time.

December 24, 1864

While I dusted, I listened to the Porter children chat again. This time, they were talking about visiting the President's House. They spoke about Tad Lincoln as if he were their friend. Tad is only ten and goes everywhere with his father. I have never seen Tad.

But I wish now with all my heart I knew him. I wish with all my soul I was him.

Never before have I wished to be someone other than myself. The Porter children have put me under a strange spell.

December 25, 1864

A snowy Christmas day. Jane Ellen stayed in bed. Pa forced himself up. He asked me if I would like to go with him to Finley Hospital tonight. He wants to play his violin for the wounded soldiers.

Later

At twilight, Pa and I tread through the wet snow and mud to the hospital. I could tell that his back ached with every step.

On the way, sleigh bells jingled on

Pennsylvania Avenue. I heard children laughing. I thought I saw the Porters ride by. Or some other family just like them. A rich, happy family.

As we entered the hospital, I heard the cries and groans of wounded soldiers. I dreaded seeing them all.

I kept my eyes down as we entered a ward. Pa stood in a corner and began to play his violin. As "Silent Night" wafted through the cold, drafty room, the cries ceased. I saw tears stream down the face of a lady nurse.

As Pa kept playing, angels seemed to calm the air. The room became warm with a deep, holy feeling.

On our walk home, I felt the angels were still with us. I heard no sleigh bells or didn't notice. For a short while, I felt peaceful and happy just to be myself.

December 26, 1864

Drizzly rain.

Hundreds of guns boomed in Franklin Square this morning. Jed told us the city is celebrating General Sherman's conquest of Savannah, Georgia. He thinks the war will end by spring.

December 27, 1864

The Porter children went home today.

I watched the servants carry their trunks out to their carriage. They received many gifts from their grandmother for Christmas. One was the very copy of *Swiss Family Robinson* that I had been reading to her.

They received other books as well — *The Tiger Prince* and *Life in the Woods*. Sarah and

Eliza left in fur-lined cloaks. Robert carried away new skates and a sled.

After they rode away, Mrs. Porter went up to her bed to lie down.

When I got home, I went straight to bed, too. Jane Ellen sat by me and stroked my hair. She asked me what was the matter, but I didn't tell her about the Porter children and their books and ribbons and dresses.

I just said I didn't feel well. When she said, "Where do you hurt?" I answered angrily, "All over!" Then I turned my face to the wall.

She seemed to understand that I did not want to talk. Forgive me, God, but my life seems quite small compared to that of the Porter children. And now I'll never know the ending of *Swiss Family Robinson.*

December 28, 1864

Tonight Jane Ellen declared that we were all too gloomy. She tried to cheer us up by saying we must think of a name for the baby.

We each suggested a few names, but we found none that all could agree upon. The conversation dwindled away, for I fear our hearts were not in it.

December 29, 1864

Mrs. Porter was still resting in bed today, so I left work early.

On my walk home, I finally saw the sight I've been waiting for — President Lincoln riding his gray horse! And Tad at his side on his own horse!

I recognized them at once when I saw all

the soldiers guarding them. The soldiers held sabers over their shoulders.

The President looked grave as he rode by. His dark eyes stared straight ahead. His face seemed even more deeply lined than when I saw him in Gettysburg.

I caught only a glimpse of Tad. He was laughing at something and looked quite happy. I was seized with such a yearning to be Tad Lincoln that I could scarcely breathe.

When I got home to our dreary rooms, I went straight to bed without hardly a word to anyone.

Never has my own family looked more tattered and wanting.

December 30, 1864

Tonight a crowd in the street was singing "When This Cruel War Is Over." Only half-listening, I thought they were singing "This Cruel World," and I'll admit I did not think it strange.

December 31, 1864

We are all together tonight. Jane Ellen served a special dinner of turkey for New Year's Eve. Jed says everyone believes 1865 will most certainly bring about the war's end.

We should be happier about this, I think. Perhaps it is the gray, rainy weather that keeps us all in such a state of melancholy.

January 1, 1865

Tomorrow, Jed, Pa, and I are going to the New Year's reception at the President's House. All the public is invited to shake hands with the President.

I will look for Tad Lincoln. I have a great urge to see him again. I consider him the luckiest boy alive.

Some nights I yearn so much to be Tad that I cannot even sleep. I shiver with cold in my bed and imagine myself riding on horseback with the President.

January 2, 1865

Everyone in the world wanted to shake the President's hand today. Pa, Jed, and I did not even get close to him. Thousands of men, ladies, and children pressed forward. The crush was so great that some were hurt.

We went home, sorely disappointed. Jane Ellen was cheered later to hear that a number of Negroes were able to meet with the President. They all exclaimed, "God bless Abraham Lincoln!"

The President is pushing for a change to the Constitution that will end slavery once and for all.

January 4, 1865

A huge snowstorm today. Freezing cold. Fighting the wind on the way to Mrs. Porter's, I almost wished I could lie down and die.

January 9, 1865

Each day, I see more deserters from the Confederate army. Jed says many have nowhere to go. On my way home this evening, I passed one who appeared to be frozen stiff. He was lying in an alley with no shoes or hat. His eyes closed, his face blue.

I wondered about my mother's two younger

brothers. Were they fighting as Rebs? Where are they now?

Does one lie somewhere on the cold ground? Or are they buried underneath it?

I wish Pa had stayed in touch with my mother's family after her death. Now we'll never know who — or where — any of them are.

Jed seems to feel as I do. Two days ago, he carried an old blanket out to a Reb sleeping on the ground near our house. He said the man could be our kin for all we know.

January 17, 1865

I have not written in my journal lately, for there has not been much to write. Mrs. Porter left last week to visit her son's family in New York City. Her maid went with her. Her elderly manservant stayed here, but he keeps to himself. I go to her house each day. But I do little more than dust and polish and embroider. In my free time, I sometimes move about the house, pretending I am Mrs. Porter's granddaughter.

January 19, 1865

I keep playing the game of pretending to be Mrs. Porter's granddaughter. When the fantasy wears thin, I stare out a window and daydream about her real grandchildren.

What exciting things are they doing now in New York City? I imagine they live in a fancy mansion and ride in sleighs and go to a fine school and many parties.

Every time I look at photographs of them, a strange grief stabs my heart. I wish their beautiful mother was mine. And their father, too, I sometimes wish was mine. Forgive me, Pa.

January 26, 1865

It is one of the coldest winters on record this year. None of us can seem to get warm. I see Pa shivering even when he is standing close to the fire.

January 30, 1865

The paper says that the famous orator Edward Everett has died. I remember him speaking at Gettysburg. I thought his speech would never end.

Now I feel a bit sad, longing for those days when we were building our lives again after the terrible battle. There was hope in the air and a feeling that we ourselves had been heroes.

Today, our family seems tattered in comparison to how we were then. Pa is so distant and seldom speaks. Jane Ellen is in bed constantly and has little good humor or happiness to share. Jed feels guilty for everyone's plight and stays late at work on purpose, I think. And I am feeling quite cross and mean.

What has happened to us? And to our great adventure in Mr. Lincoln's Washington?

January 31, 1865

Jane Ellen got up from bed today. She wrote to her Negro friend, Becky Lee, in Gettysburg, to tell her congratulations.

Congress has voted to pass the Thirteenth Amendment to abolish slavery. Now it must go to the states for something called "ratification." Then it will be the law of the land. Becky Lee will soon be legally free forever.

Amen, says Jane Ellen.

How, I wonder, could a people have ever allowed slavery? The evil of it seems so clear. I can only think that, throughout history, most children have held doubts about slavery in their hearts. But children become used to the customs of their time and place. As they grow older, they forget their doubts and follow in the footsteps of their parents and grandparents. Now, for the first time, our whole nation is about to start down a new path together.

February 1, 1865

I saw an interesting ad in the paper today.

It said, "How can you find wealth and good fortune? Find out from Madame Masha at

402 K Street. For ten cents, she tells the future and gives good advice to young and old."

I would love some good advice. More than that, I would love to know my future.

February 6, 1865

I was paid today for the last two weeks of work. As usual, I handed my money over to Pa — all except ten cents.

Pa did not notice, for he never counts what I give him. It hurts his pride too much. He just drops the paper in the cookie jar without looking.

I kept the ten-cent paper note so I can go see Madame Masha, first chance I get. I do not feel guilty about keeping the money from the others. I am desperate for advice on how to find wealth and good fortune for all of us.

February 15, 1865

Today, Pa sent me to the store for bread. I hurried and bought the bread. Then I ran all the way to 402 K Street. I tapped on Madame Masha's door, and she let me in.

She wore a beautiful lavender dress. She had a red scarf tied around her hair. And sweet-smelling candles burned throughout the room.

She asked me why I had come. I told her I needed to know how I could find wealth and good fortune.

Madame Masha looked deeply into my eyes for a long moment. Then she picked up my hand and studied my palm.

"Ah, this is serious," she said. "You have allowed the goddess Envy to attack you."

Horrified, I asked what she meant.

She said wherever Envy strikes, the sun no longer shines. All flowers die. One feels cold and cannot sleep.

"That's right," I whispered. Madame Masha knew exactly how I'd been feeling since I'd met the Porter children!

She said the goddess Envy had placed a nest of thorns in my heart.

I quickly put my hand over my heart, for it hurt even as she said this.

What can I do? I asked.

She told me I must banish Envy completely. I must post guards at the doors to my heart and mind. I must not let Envy enter again, she told me. Not for an instant.

"Or she will smite all the love in you," she said.

I nodded and felt so afraid I could scarcely breathe. When I found my voice again, I asked about Pa, Jane Ellen, and Jed. Could Madame

Masha tell me what was going to happen to them?

She nodded slowly. "Great change is coming," she said, "great change is coming."

I was very relieved to hear this.

Then she said, "Now go home and take your bread back to your family."

Goodness! How did she know the bread was for my family?

I gave her ten cents. Then I ran all the way home. I ran as if my family's lives depended on the bread I was carrying.

As I ran, my heart felt as if it might burst. I had a horrible fear that my family might not be there when I got home. I feared I might have lost them all. The goddess Envy might have slain them already!

When I came through the door, relief flooded over me. Everyone seemed fine. Jane Ellen was reading the newspaper. Pa was writing out some music. Jed was boiling water for coffee.

I broke into tears, and everyone looked at me with alarm.

"I'm sorry!" I cried out. "I've been terrible and mean, and I'm sorry! I love you all! Please forgive me! Please!"

I threw myself onto Pa and cried my heart out. He just held me tightly as I tried to explain how I had envied Mrs. Porter's grandchildren and how I had wanted to go to the theater and have fancy clothes and a beautiful house. I told them that I had been feeling mean and spiteful. And I was so sorry!

Pa gently helped me onto the sofa. He covered me with a blanket and told me he'd always love me no matter what I felt or did. He told me he never thought of me as mean and spiteful. He said I always seemed brave and kind to him.

Then Jed sat with me. He said he imag-
ined that Abraham Lincoln himself must
have felt great envy as a child. After all, his
family had been very poor. His mother had
died, and he'd lived in a humble log cabin. But
look at him today, Jed said. He is the most
powerful person in all the land. His envy did
not harm him at all. "And it will not harm
you," he said.

Later, Jane Ellen sat beside me and stroked
my hair. She said that she understood quite
well how I had been feeling. She said that she
herself felt envy at times. She said we are only
human and that God loves us even when we
are full of discontent. She said God waits
patiently for us to discover the wealth of love
around us.

I clutched Jane Ellen's soft hand and held it
to my cheek. And the greatest joy came over
me. Not only was my family not harmed by my

meanness, they all understood it in their own way. And they all loved me no matter what.

I felt like the richest girl in the world.

February 17, 1865

Jed just got home and told us that the Union army has captured Columbia, South Carolina. The Confederate government in Richmond is starting to fall apart, too. The war may end soon.

This news has made me, Pa, Jed, and Jane Ellen happy. Tonight we all talked excitedly and looked at the map, and tried to figure out when the Confederates might surrender.

February 18, 1865

Hundreds of Confederates are deserting each day. They are flocking to Washington, eager to swear loyalty to the Union. On my way to and from work, I see them sleeping in the streets and alleyways. They look horribly worn and beaten down. It will be a great relief to everyone when we are one country again.

February 20, 1865

I feel as if I have just recovered from a bad illness. I work quickly in Mrs. Porter's house. I do not look at her grandchildren's photographs. I do not stare out the window and daydream about their lives. I race home each night to the ones I love.

I do not want Envy to attack me again and plant thorns in my heart.

February 21, 1865

Great news. Soon Jed will have a better job at the newspaper! Mr. Hoke has finally returned from Georgia. He was angry to learn that Jed had not been made a reporter right away. He said, "What a waste of great talent!"

Mr. Hoke promised that Jed will be writing news stories very soon.

We are all so happy about this change of events. Pa played his fiddle tonight, and we danced.

February 22, 1865

The last Confederate port in Wilmington, North Carolina, has fallen to Union forces.

February 23, 1865

The good news about Jed's job seems to have put a fire under Pa. He is planning to leave the house today for the first time in weeks. He says he will carry his violin around the city, looking for work again.

Evening

Pa just came home. He was in jolly spirits. He learned that Professor Withers, the orchestra conductor at Ford's New Theatre, will be holding auditions for a new violin player next week!

I pray to God and my mother in heaven to help Pa get the job.

February 28, 1865

We all had a cheerful discussion tonight about what to name our baby. If it's a girl, we thought it would be nice to name her after my mother, Elizabeth. If it's a boy, we thought perhaps Jonathan or Thomas. These two names are not for anyone in particular, just names that all four of us happen to like.

March 1, 1865

Hurrah! Pa got the job! He will be a violin player in Professor Withers's orchestra!

Our happiness had no bounds tonight. Pa played his violin, and Jed and I danced. Jane Ellen could only wave her arms, for she is quite big now.

Pa wants me to stop working at once.

I feel a pang of sorrow leaving Mrs. Porter.

But in truth, I have not seen her very much recently, as she has been spending a great deal of time in New York City.

I will give notice tomorrow. And I will go back to having school lessons with Jane Ellen. Pa says that by next year, I will be in a fine school.

Surprisingly, Jane Ellen feels better now. Though far along in her pregnancy, she no longer gets sick to her stomach. She laughs whenever she feels our baby kicking.

Great changes *have* come to all of us recently. Madame Masha is a genius!

March 2, 1865

Mrs. Porter was quite lovely about my leaving her employment. She wished me the best of luck and said I was a most admirable girl.

I'm glad she never knew how much I envied her grandchildren. She would have thought less of me, I fear.

March 3, 1865

Pa learned the most wonderful news of all today: He will be a substitute violin player with the Finley Hospital Band at the second inaugural ball! Their violin player is ill, so Pa will take his place just for the night.

The ball will be held at the Patent Office. Four thousand people are expected to attend!

And Jed will be reporting on the inauguration ceremony for the newspaper!

Great changes keep coming into our lives! Thank you, Madame Masha.

Later

The town is crowded with people coming for the inauguration ceremony tomorrow.

Gloomy wet skies all day. But Pa and I went for a walk after dark. We heard bands playing lively music. Torches burned through the evening mist. On the roof of the Capitol a silver light shined on the American flag.

March 4, 1865

An early morning storm swept through the city, uprooting trees.

The dark clouds and wind did not stop us from going to see President Lincoln sworn in. Hundreds of people, including me and Pa, waded in the mud to the Capitol.

The steps of the Capitol were well guarded.

Only the press — including Jed — were allowed to stand on them.

Later, Jed told us that guards were also posted at roads and bridges, watching for sneaky-looking characters.

The President looked quite splendid in his plain black suit and white gloves.

By the time he spoke, the rain had stopped. The sun was shining. He called for a "just and lasting peace." He said we should "bind up the nation's wounds."

He kissed the Bible. Then he rode back to his mansion with Tad by his side.

I kept my own guards close by and would not allow that monster Envy to come near me. I was glad for Tad Lincoln. And for all of us. Abraham Lincoln is our father, too. He is the father of this whole nation.

March 5, 1865

Jed went to the White House last night to report on the reception for the President. He said hoards of people rushed in to shake hands with President Lincoln. As many as 6,000!

Now Jed's worrying about the President again. Jed said he looked feeble and thin.

March 6, 1865

Tonight, Pa plays at the inaugural ball. I begged him to let me go with him. He said I could not, but he'll wake me when he returns and will tell me all about it.

I told him to keep his eye out for Tad Lincoln.

Later

Thousands of people went to the ball, Pa said. The band played waltzes and polkas. The ladies wore yellow and blue silk dresses. Their curls were powdered with silver dust.

Pa said everyone was especially cheerful. They all seem to believe the war will end very soon. "Imagine, the Patent Office was used for a hospital during the worst time of fighting," said Pa. "But tonight it was filled with music and lovely ladies."

When Pa spoke of the ladies, he sounded quite wistful. I think they reminded him of my mother. He met her long ago at a dance, when she wore a lovely gown and he was playing the violin.

Pa said everyone danced and danced. By the time the midnight supper was served, some guests had become too merry — they behaved in the wildest manner. They pounced on the food! They snatched whole chickens from the table! The floor became littered with cakes and broken dishes and glasses. There was even a big brawl in the kitchen, Pa said.

Pa never caught sight of Tad Lincoln, nor President and Mrs. Lincoln. But he said that it was a party he will never forget.

March 10, 1865

Every day more and more Rebs desert the Confederate army. They are all streaming into Washington. Pa and Jane Ellen think the war will end soon. The South has no more men to fight for it.

I must do all the cooking now. Jane Ellen is too tired to stand, and Pa and Jed are working long hours.

I do not mind. The days are getting longer

and warmer. There are buds on the cherry trees, and there is hope in the air.

There is hope in our household, too. I feel it whenever I look at Jane Ellen. Seven more weeks and our baby will be born.

March 13, 1865

Jed saw President Lincoln today. He was riding in his carriage with Tad!

The President definitely needs a holiday, Jed said. He still looks very weary and thin.

March 20, 1865

I've not written in my journal for a week. I have been so busy. I must do all the housework and shopping now, as well as the cooking.

Our baby is due in less than six weeks. Jane Ellen is so big, she does not leave the house at all. She moves very carefully and seems very thoughtful. This morning I overheard her talking in a soothing voice.

"Do not worry," she whispered. "The world will love you and embrace you when you come."

She is right. I don't think a little baby will ever be more welcomed. I pray every night for Jane Ellen to be safe, and our baby, too.

April 3, 1865

Today newsboys shouted, "Richmond has fallen! The capital of the Confederacy in ruins! Union troops have taken over the city!"

People cheered in the streets.

Pa is playing with the orchestra at Ford's New Theatre tonight. He said that the audience will be in a great mood.

Pa loves playing at the theater and being a part of the plays. He seems very merry now.

April 4, 1865

Outside our windows tonight, we hear people still shouting in the twilight: "Richmond is ours! Glory hallelujah!"

We hear the ringing of bells and band music playing. A steam fire engine barreled by a moment ago. It was blasting off steam in celebration of the fall of the capital of the Confederacy.

At dinner, Jed told us that people swarmed into the newspaper office today. They grabbed all the papers with the latest news.

Jed said President Lincoln and his son Tad have gone to Richmond. He heard that many Negroes knelt before the President to thank him for freeing them from slavery. But President Lincoln told them not to kneel before him. "You must kneel to God only and thank him for your freedom," he said.

The war is not over yet, Jed said. Many lives may still be lost.

When Jane Ellen told Jed to stop being so gloomy, he only shook his head sadly.

I wish Jed had a lighter heart. I fear the Battle of Gettysburg scarred him forever.

April 5, 1865

The city is filling up with thousands of deserters from the Confederate army. Jed says the South now has fewer than 100,000 soldiers, while the North has a million.

Everyone is trying to guess when General Robert E. Lee will surrender.

April 7, 1865

On my way to the city market this morning, the dogwood trees along Pennsylvania Avenue were filled with blossoms.

Through the pink, dappled light I saw a carriage go by — the Porter children were riding inside! I imagine they are visiting Mrs. Porter for the Easter holidays.

I am glad to say I did not feel at all empty when I saw them. I did not dwell on their good fortune and riches. I banished even the temptation of thinking such thoughts.

When I got to the market, I filled my basket with strawberries. Also with apples, cheese, and fine brown sugar. It is fun to shop now with a little extra money.

On the way home, I saw a Confederate band leading a group of deserters through the city. All the traffic had come to a stop. The band played "Ain't We Glad to Get Out of the Wilderness"!

I feel that I, too, have come out of a wilderness, the wilderness of Resentment and Envy.

April 8, 1865

Night and day, Pa is practicing a new song composed by Professor Withers for the orchestra. It's called "Honor to Our Soldiers."

The orchestra will play it on Friday night at Ford's New Theatre, when Miss Laura Keene will be starring in *Our American Cousin*. Pa said he might be able to sneak me into the back of the theater, as it will be Miss Keene's last performance.

Imagine! Ford's New Theatre — where the Porter children saw *Rip Van Winkle*! I wish they would be in the audience when I'm there.

I wish they would see me leaving with my father — *a violinist in the orchestra!*

Oh dear, I am coming under Envy's spell again. Now I want others to envy *me*.

Forgive me, Madame Masha.

April 9, 1865

I am baking an apple pie for our Palm Sunday dinner.

Jed must work all day. He has to wait to receive news from the telegraph office about the possible surrender of General Robert E. Lee today.

Later

Jed just came in. He was overjoyed — and for Jed, that is saying a lot. He told us General Lee has surrendered! He and General Grant met in Appomattox, Virginia, today, and Lee surrendered his army.

Finally, the war is over!

April 10, 1865

Early this morning, the whole city got the news about General Lee's surrender. The morning paper headline said: "Hang Out Your Banners! Union Victory! Peace!"

By noon, flags waved in the rain all up and down our street.

A great crowd gathered outside the White House. President Lincoln appeared, bright and happy. He told the band to play "Dixie." He said that "Dixie" belongs to all of us again and not just to the South.

A while ago, Pa played "Dixie" himself, and Jed and I danced around the room. Jane Ellen burst into tears. All she could say was, "We are one nation again. We are *all* free — black and white."

April 11, 1865

More rain today. But we are still so joyous, it seems that the sun is shining.

Later

Great news! Pa says I can go to the theater with him on Good Friday to see Miss Laura Keene's last performance! All 1,000 seats will be filled, but I can stand in the back, Pa says.

I am trembling with excitement. I sense that I might love the theater more than anything else. Beautiful Miss Laura Keene — the actors and actresses — the costumes — the lights and music!

But what will I wear? I have shot up like a

beanpole in the past few months. My one good dress no longer fits me.

April 12, 1865

Jane Ellen is a saint. She is giving me one of her nicest dresses to wear to Ford's New Theatre on Good Friday. Even though it strains her to sit up, she has promised to stitch the dress to make it smaller at the waist, and she will sew the hem.

Tomorrow night the city will have a Grand Illumination. All the government buildings and homes will be lit up with gas lights. Pa will play with the orchestra on the Capitol steps.

Except for the week we found Jed in the field hospital, these are the greatest days of our lives!

April 13, 1865

Tonight, if you had been an angel looking down from heaven, you would have thought Washington City was one giant flame. You might have even thought the whole world was on fire.

The night was as light as day. Music played and flags waved. Walking past all the bright lamps with Jed and Pa, I thought, "This is the most joyous city on all the earth."

And best of all, my joy will not end. Tomorrow is Good Friday, and I am going to the theater for the very first time. And in just two weeks, our baby will be born.

April 14, 1865

It is cold and windy this Good Friday. Dark clouds hover overhead. I only pray it doesn't rain, so that I won't get my "new" dress muddy tonight. It is soft yellow with lovely lace. When I wear it, I feel like a young lady and not a child.

Jane Ellen spent some time this morning practicing on my hair. Tonight, she is going to sweep it all up in a bun. I don't think Pa and Jed will even recognize me!

Early evening

I am not going to the theater. Pa said I can't because the afternoon newspaper announced that President Lincoln and his wife have decided at the last moment to go see Miss Laura Keene's final performance.

Pa said security will be very tight. He will not be able to sneak me in.

I cried and carried on after he told me this. Jed and Jane Ellen both tried to comfort me.

Through my tears, I told them that I know I

can go to Ford's New Theatre someday in the future. But I wish it were tonight — when the President himself will be there! That would be a dream beyond all my dreams! Maybe even Tad will be there. Maybe I could even have met them because my father plays in the orchestra!

Jed promised me that he will take me to the President's House someday when he covers a story there.

I refused to cheer up, though. I still feel most angry and ungrateful.

Late night

I write with a trembling hand. Pa just came home. A terrible calamity took place at the theater tonight. President Lincoln was shot.

The man who shot him leaped from the President's box onto the stage. He rushed into the wings, then vanished outside. He jumped on a horse in the alleyway and dashed away in the dark.

Pa did not know who the man was.

Mrs. Lincoln started to scream. Soldiers cleared the theater. They carried the bleeding President to a nearby house. He had been shot in the head.

Pa and Jane Ellen and Jed are all weeping. I am writing so I will not lose my mind.

How can this be?

Dear God, spare the life of President Lincoln, please, dear God. He is the father of our nation.

Clouds cover the moon. The night is so dark, it feels like every candle on earth has gone out.

Before dawn

I have not slept. Jed left after midnight to go to the newspaper. He was in a fever of anxiety. I am very worried about Jane Ellen and Pa.

Pa seems a bit out of his head. For hours he has been pacing the floor, as he did long ago when he discovered Jed was missing in Gettysburg. I hear him talking to my mother in heaven. He is telling her to pray for our fallen leader.

Jane Ellen sobs loudly from her bed. I fear for our baby who is to be born in a week.

I am waiting desperately for news from Jed. I refuse to think the President will die. God will not let him die.

April 15, 1865

Jed returned briefly after dawn. He spoke softly, as if he dared not hear his own cruel words. He said President Lincoln is sinking rapidly. He cannot live much longer. The

President was shot by an actor named John Wilkes Booth. The assassin has not been caught yet.

After he told us the news, Jed wept. Jane Ellen held him and wept, too. Pa and I wept. We all wept and prayed together.

Evening

President Lincoln is dead.

Soldiers and man-hunters are searching the land for John Wilkes Booth.

A cold rain is falling. The sky weeps rain, as it did the morning after the Battle of Gettysburg.

This seems like a terrible dream. I still cannot believe it's true.

We keep weeping. All of us. Our hearts are broken.

April 16, 1865
Easter Sunday

Our minister, Reverend Crane, said that the President died for our country just as Christ died for the world.

He said that John Wilkes Booth will not escape. The assassin might try to hide in the remotest place. But he will be found. Wherever he is, he will be found.

I still cannot believe our President is lost to us forever. I can't believe he will never lead his people again. Or ride by on his horse. Or stand at the window of his mansion.

Pa has stopped speaking. He is mute with anger and grief.

April 17, 1865

Jane Ellen is not well. I am desperately afraid for the baby. It is due within the week, but I fear Jane Ellen is so filled with sorrow, she will not have enough strength to bring new life into this world.

I tried to interest her in the baby today by asking her what we will name him if he is a boy. We have not yet chosen between Jonathan and Thomas. But she just turned her face to the wall and said she did not care.

Jed stays at the newspaper, and Pa wanders sadly about the city.

I sit at the window, waiting for them both to come home. They must help me comfort Jane Ellen. If anything happens to our baby, that will surely be the end of all of us.

April 18, 1865

All the houses up and down the street are draped in black. Pa is leaving soon to go view the President's body at the President's House. Thousands are already lined up there, Jed says.

I told Jed that he should stay home for the sake of Jane Ellen and our unborn baby. He is anxious about her, too. But he said he must report the story about the President's funeral. I could see Jed was greatly upset, so I tried to calm him. I told him not to worry — I would take care of Jane Ellen.

April 19, 1865

Bells toll all over the city.

The sun is blazing today. The cheerful brightness seems to mock our sorrow. It is the day of our President's funeral procession.

On Friday, the train will leave to carry his body back to his hometown in Springfield, Illinois, to be buried. The train will pass through many cities, and thousands of people will see it go by.

Later

Pa could barely speak when he returned home. But Jed described what he saw to Jane Ellen and me.

He said the procession moved slowly down Pennsylvania Avenue to the Capitol. Many thousands took part in the march.

A funeral carriage carried the President's remains. It was draped in black.

Behind the carriage was the President's gray horse. The horse carried no rider.

When Jed told us about the riderless horse, I burst into tears. I felt so sad for the gray horse missing his lost rider. I felt sad for Tad Lincoln missing the father who once rode beside him.

April 20, 1865

There is a $100,000 reward for the capture of John Wilkes Booth, the President's murderer.

Jed says the South will not give shelter to John Wilkes Booth, wherever he is. The South is grieving much like the North, says Jed. Many Southerners think Lincoln was their friend, too. At the war's end, he chose the path of forgiveness instead of revenge.

Jed said that Lincoln once said in a speech that we must all be friends, not enemies. The President had called up the "better angels of our nature" to help us.

I think only our better angels can help my family now. We are all still so sad, we barely speak to one another. Each of us seems locked in a private room of grief.

April 23, 1865

Jane Ellen is in great pain. She is tossing about on the bed and crying out. Jed is with her, holding her hands and talking gently. Pa has run out to the street to get a carriage to take her to the hospital.

It is pouring rain. I pray, I pray, I pray that Pa can find a carriage soon.

Later

Still pouring rain. Thunder booms in the sky. We are waiting at the hospital. Jane Ellen is in the operating room. Jed is pale and quiet and stares out the window. Pa is pacing the floor, whispering to himself, as if asking my mother in heaven for help.

I am writing in my journal, to keep from losing my mind.

Dear God, help us.

Early morning

Pa and I just got home. Jed is staying with Jane Ellen — and our new baby boy.

Jane Ellen gave birth around midnight.

She bled a great deal. But the lady nurses stopped the blood and said she would be fine. They said the baby would be fine, too.

Pa and I are dead tired. But we are happy. For the first time in many days, our spirits are lifted. On the way home we talked about all the things we'll do with the baby as he grows up. Pa wants to teach him how to play the violin. I want to read books to him and teach him his letters.

The weather has cleared up. The brightest sunlight pours through our windows now, after the rain.

April 24, 1865

The baby looks quite red and tiny. He is sleeping peacefully at Jane Ellen's side. She is sleeping peacefully, too, though she looks very pale.

I don't want to leave them. I've been sitting here all morning, staring at their sweet faces.

Jane Ellen is going to live. My mother died, but Jane Ellen did not die. Our baby will have a wonderful mother.

April 25, 1865

Jane Ellen and our baby came home today. The doctors said she must stay in bed for at least two weeks. All of us must help take care of the baby — especially me, since Pa and Jed will be working.

Jed is so happy. For the first time since the President's death, he is moving about briskly and talking and making plans. He says we'll all name the baby tomorrow. Jane Ellen is too weary to think of a name today.

April 26, 1865

We have named the baby.

Pa, Jed, Jane Ellen, and I each wrote down on a piece of paper the name we most wanted. When we held up our papers, we saw that everyone had written the very same name: Abraham Lincoln Dickens.

What a big name for a tiny boy. He has a funny little face that makes silly expressions. His eyes stay closed, but his small hands grasp my finger and hold on tightly.

I am in love with him.

April 27, 1865

Jed just came home and told us that yesterday the Union cavalry trapped John Wilkes Booth in a barn. He was shot in the head and died. Other conspirators are being sought.

April 28, 1865

When I look at our tiny baby, I think about the day President Lincoln was born. It is hard to imagine that he was once such a tiny baby as ours. Did his mother ever dream he would be a great man?

May 1, 1865

I don't have much time to write in my journal now. I am always helping with the baby.

May 4, 1865

The baby is sleeping. For a quick moment, I am free to write.

Today the President was buried in Springfield,

Illinois. His funeral train passed thousands of weeping mourners along the way.

I feel great sorrow for our whole nation. But most of all, I feel sorrow for Tad Lincoln. Just a few months ago, I thought he was the luckiest boy in the world. Now I think he must be the saddest.

I thought Madame Masha was an amazing fortune-teller. When she said, "Great change is coming," I thought she had special knowledge about the future.

The truth is Madame Masha only told me what is always true. Great change is *always* taking place. One day we envy someone. The next day, we pity the same person. One day a great man dies. The next, a tiny baby is born. One day there's rain. The next, the sun shines brightly.

If change is always taking place, how can

we live a happy life? How can we not be fearful all the time?

Maybe all we can do is try to keep hope in our hearts — try to trust "the better angels of our nature" to hold us together.

I must close now, as Jane Ellen needs my help. Abraham Lincoln Dickens has just woken up.

Life in America
in 1864

Historical Note

The Civil War began in 1861 because of many differences between the Northern and Southern states. The North had outlawed slavery, but the South depended upon black slaves to work on its plantations. Southerners wanted to make their own laws. This led to the "War Between the States," or the Civil War.

In the winter of 1864–65, Washington, D.C., the nation's capital, was filled with thousands of bedraggled soldiers escaping the final months of the Civil War. Washington was not a modern city. It was filled with shabby, neglected buildings. It had dirty, unpaved

Houses on the outskirts of Washington, D.C.

streets and no proper sewage system. Pigs and cows wandered around freely. People caught diseases from bad water and from the mosquitoes that lived in the stagnant swamps around the city.

Abraham and Tad Lincoln.

In November 1864, Abraham Lincoln was elected to his second term as president. President Lincoln had risen from humble beginnings to become one of the nation's most revered presidents. His strength and wisdom had guided the Union through four terrible years of the war. After the Battle of Gettysburg in 1863, he called upon the American people to dedicate themselves to the task of preserving a nation, "of the people, by the people, for the people."

The job now before Lincoln was tremendous: He wanted the Civil War to end. He wanted slavery to end. And he wanted the country to unite peacefully again, as one nation, one family, and "to bind up its wounds."

General Lee surrenders to General Grant at Appomattox Courthouse.

In 1865, Lincoln began to see some of his hopes realized. In late January, Congress passed the Thirteenth Amendment to the Constitution, abolishing the practice of slavery. And on Palm Sunday, April 9, in Appomattox, Virginia, General Robert E. Lee, leader of the Confederate army, surrendered to General Ulysses S. Grant, leader of the Union forces.

In the days following Lee's surrender, the United States celebrated the end of the Civil War with wild jubilation. The streets of Washington were filled with music and fireworks.

Ford's New Theatre.

The celebrating, though, soon turned to terrible shock and grief. On Good Friday, just five days after Lee's surrender, President Lincoln was shot while attending a play at Ford's

New Theatre. He died the next day. His assassin was John Wilkes Booth, a sympathizer for the Confederate cause.

Booth had murdered the one man who was most capable of helping the nation to bind up its wounds. The loss of Abraham Lincoln was mourned by the North and South alike.

John Wilkes Booth.

About the Author

Mary Pope Osborne says, "I have a strong personal connection to Ford's Theatre in Washington, D.C., the theater where Abraham Lincoln was assassinated in 1865. Many years ago, I first saw my husband, Will, when he was starring in a play there. We later met and were married. Working on this book, I had the opportunity to revisit the theater that held such good memories for me, and such tragic memories for our nation."

Mary Pope Osborne is the award-winning author of many books for children, including the best-selling Magic Tree House series;

Adaline Falling Star; a My America book: *My Brother's Keeper;* and two Dear America books: *Standing in the Light* and *My Secret War.* She lives with her husband, Will, in New York City.

Acknowledgments

With special thanks to Amy Griffin, Beth Levine, Diane Garvey Nesin, and Dwayne Howard.

Grateful acknowledgment is made for permission to reprint the following:

Cover portrait and frontispiece by Glenn Harrington.

Page 102 (top): Houses on the outskirts of Washington, D.C., Historical Society of Washington, D.C.
Page 102 (bottom): Abraham and Tad Lincoln, North Wind Picture Archives.
Page 103: General Lee surrenders to General Grant at Appomattox Courthouse, Superstock.
Page 104: Ford's New Theatre, North Wind Picture Archives.
Page 105: John Wilkes Booth, Brown Brothers.

Other books in the My America series

Corey's Underground Railroad Diaries
by Sharon Dennis Wyeth
Book One: Freedom's Wings
Book Two: Flying Free

Elizabeth's Jamestown Colony Diaries
by Patricia Hermes
Book One: Our Strange New Land
Book Two: The Starving Time

Hope's Revolutionary War Diaries
by Kristiana Gregory
Book One: Five Smooth Stones
Book Two: We Are Patriots

Joshua's Oregon Trail Diaries
by Patricia Hermes
Book One: Westward to Home

Virginia's Civil War Diaries
by Mary Pope Osborne
Book One: My Brother's Keeper

To Dr. Jack Hrkach,
with love and gratitude

⊶⇒ ⇐⊷

While the events described and some of the characters in this book may be based on actual historical events and real people, Virginia Dickens is a fictional character, created by the author, and her diary is a work of fiction.

Copyright © 2001 by Mary Pope Osborne

Library of Congress Cataloging-in-Publication Data
Pope Osborne, Mary.
After the Rain: Virginia's Diary, Book Two / by Mary Pope Osborne
ISBN 0-439-20138-1; 0-439-36904-5 (pbk.)
p. cm. — (My America)
Summary: In her diary, a ten-year-old girl writes about her family's experiences living in
Washington, D.C., in 1864–5, during which time the Civil War comes to an end and
President Lincoln is assassinated. Includes historical notes.
[1. Lincoln, Abraham, 1809–1865 — Fiction. 2. Diaries — Fiction. 3. Washington
(D.C.) — History — Civil War, 1861–1865 — Juvenile fiction. 4. Washington (D.C.) —
History — Civil War, 1861–1865 — Fiction. 5. United States — History —
Civil War, 1861–1865 — Fiction.] I. Title. II. Series.
PZ7.081167 Ah 2002
[Fic] — 21 00-020200
CIP AC

10 9 8 7 6 5 4   04 05

The display type was set in Colwell Roman.
The text type was set in Goudy.
Photo research by Zoe Moffitt
Book design by Elizabeth B. Parisi

Printed in the U.S.A.
First paperback edition, May 2002

⊶⇒ ⇐⊷